# Dear Parent:

Congratulations! Your child is taking the first steps on an exciting journey. The destination? Independent reading!

**STEP INTO READING®** will help your child get there. The program offers five steps to reading success. Each step includes fun stories and colorful art. There are also Step into Reading Sticker Books, Step into Reading Math Readers, Step into Reading Write-In Readers, Step into Reading Phonics Readers, and Step into Reading Phonics First Steps! Boxed Sets—a complete literacy program with something for every child.

## Learning to Read, Step by Step!

**Ready to Read**   Preschool–Kindergarten
• big type and easy words • rhyme and rhythm • picture clues
For children who know the alphabet and are eager to begin reading.

**Reading with Help**   Preschool–Grade 1
• basic vocabulary • short sentences • simple stories
For children who recognize familiar words and sound out new words with help.

**Reading on Your Own**   Grades 1–3
• engaging characters • easy-to-follow plots • popular topics
For children who are ready to read on their own.

**Reading Paragraphs**   Grades 2–3
• challenging vocabulary • short paragraphs • exciting stories
For newly independent readers who read simple sentences with confidence.

**Ready for Chapters**   Grades 2–4
• chapters • longer paragraphs • full-color art
For children who want to take the plunge into chapter books but still like colorful pictures.

**STEP INTO READING®** is designed to give every child a successful reading experience. The grade levels are only guides. Children can progress through the steps at their own speed, developing confidence in their reading, no matter what their grade.

Remember, a lifetime love of reading starts with a single step!

P9-CND-024

*For Mom, with love*
*—M.L.*

www.stepintoreading.com
www.randomhouse.com/kids/disney

Educators and librarians, for a variety of teaching tools, visit us at
www.randomhouse.com/teachers

*Library of Congress Cataloging-in-Publication Data*
Lagonegro, Melissa.
Ballerina princess / Melissa Lagonegro. — 1st ed.
    p. cm. — (Step into reading. Step 2 book)
Summary: Five Disney princesses dream of being ballerinas in separate, easy-to-read vignettes.
    ISBN-13: 978-0-7364-2428-8
    ISBN-13: 978-0-7364-8051-2 (lib. bdg.)
[1. Ballet—Fiction. 2. Dreams—Fiction. 3. Princesses—Fiction.]
I. Title. II. Series.
PZ7.L14317Bal 2007        [E]—dc22        2006009730

Printed in the United States of America    10   9   8   7

STEP INTO READING® STEP 2

DISNEY PRINCESS

By Melissa Lagonegro
Illustrated by Niall Harding

Random House 🏠 New York

A princess loves
to dream
about dancing.

She spins.

She twirls.

She moves
as if she is
floating on air.

Snow White meets
a handsome prince.

The happy couple
dances and spins.

What a lovely pair!

Belle has sweet
dancing dreams.

Belle stands
on her toes.
She holds her
arms high.

She leaps
into the air.

Belle shines
like a star.
Her dress sparkles.

One leg is up.

One leg is down.

She holds her pose.

Aurora daydreams about her dancing costume.

Should she wear
a tutu or a gown?

Cinderella dances
at the royal ball
in her dreams.

She twirls and whirls
across the floor.

Prince Charming
watches
Cinderella.

The Prince takes
her hand.
He asks her to dance.

They glide
across the room.
The guests
clap and cheer.

Ariel dreams
about dancing
with Prince Eric.
If only she had feet!

Spin and twirl
and jump!

Turn and leap
and prance!

# A princess loves to dance!